Dear Parent:

Congratulations! Your child is taking the first steps on an exciting journey. The destination? Independent reading!

STEP INTO READING® will help your child get there. The program offers five steps to reading success. Each step includes fun stories and colorful art. There are also Step into Reading Sticker Books, Step into Reading Math Readers, Step into Reading Phonics Readers, Step into Reading Write-In Readers, and Step into Reading Phonics Boxed Sets—a complete literacy program with something to interest every child.

Learning to Read, Step by Step!

Ready to Read   Preschool–Kindergarten
• big type and easy words • rhyme and rhythm • picture clues
For children who know the alphabet and are eager to begin reading.

Reading with Help   Preschool–Grade 1
• basic vocabulary • short sentences • simple stories
For children who recognize familiar words and sound out new words with help.

Reading on Your Own   Grades 1–3
• engaging characters • easy-to-follow plots • popular topics
For children who are ready to read on their own.

Reading Paragraphs   Grades 2–3
• challenging vocabulary • short paragraphs • exciting stories
For newly independent readers who read simple sentences with confidence.

Ready for Chapters   Grades 2–4
• chapters • longer paragraphs • full-color art
For children who want to take the plunge into chapter books but still like colorful pictures.

STEP INTO READING® is designed to give every child a successful reading experience. The grade levels are only guides. Children can progress through the steps at their own speed, developing confidence in their reading, no matter what their grade.

Remember, a lifetime love of reading starts with a single step!

Special thanks to Vicki Jaeger, Monica Okazaki, Kathleen Warner, Emily Kelly,
Sarah Quesenberry, Julia Phelps, Tanya Mann, Rob Hudnut, Tiffany J. Shuttleworth,
M. Elizabeth Hughes, Carla Alford, Angus Cameron, Walter P. Martishius, Tulin Ulkutay,
and Ayse Ulkutay

Visit us on the Web!
StepIntoReading.com
www.randomhouse.com/kids
www.barbie.com

Educators and librarians, for a variety of teaching tools, visit us at
www.randomhouse.com/teachers

ISBN: 978-0-375-86775-0 (trade) — ISBN: 978-0-375-96775-7 (lib. bdg.)
Printed in the United States of America   10

Barbie
A fairy secret

Adapted by Christy Webster

Based on the original screenplay by Elise Allen

Illustrated by Ulkutay Design Group

Random House 🏠 New York

Barbie is a movie star.

She has many fans.

Raquelle is her costar.

She wants to be the star.

She rips Barbie's dress!

Carrie and Taylor
help Barbie.
They fix her dress.
It happens so fast!
It seems like magic.

The next day,
Barbie sees Raquelle.
They argue.
Carrie, Taylor,
and Ken watch.

Just then,
two fairies appear.
They take Ken away!

Carrie and Taylor
are fairies, too!
They tell Barbie about
a secret fairy city.

The other fairies
took Ken there.
Graciella the fairy
princess wants
to marry Ken!

In the fairy city,
Graciella is
under a love
spell.

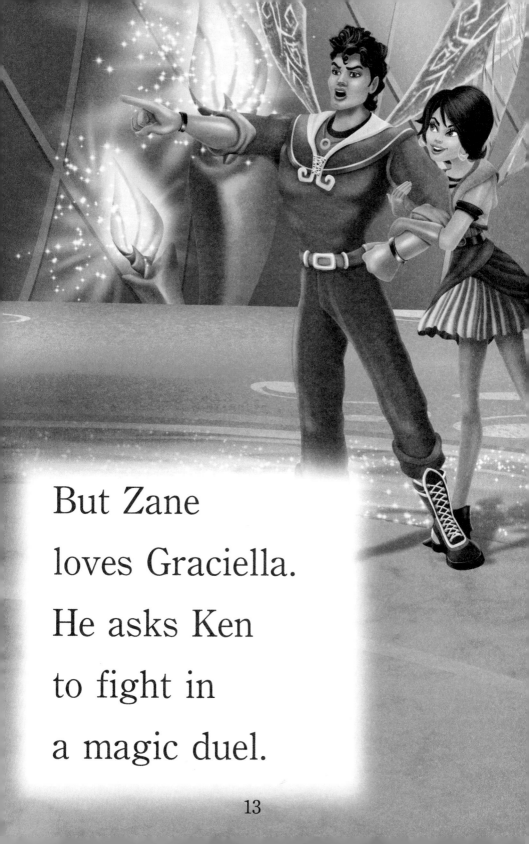

But Zane
loves Graciella.
He asks Ken
to fight in
a magic duel.

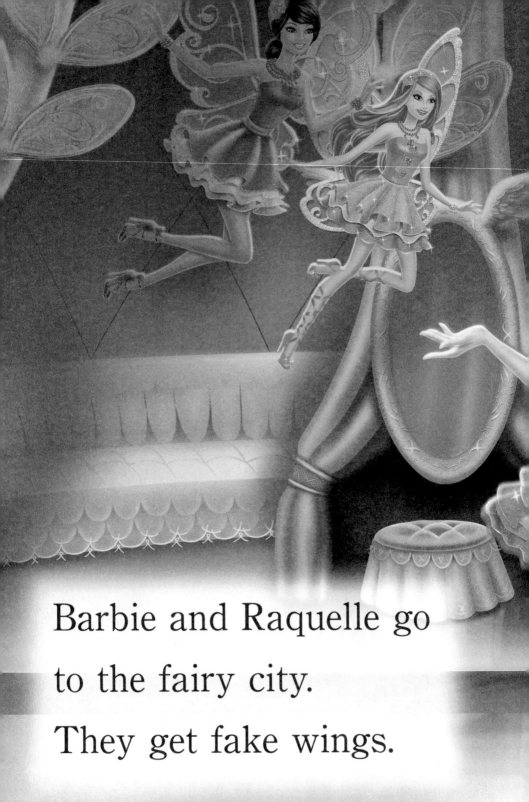

Barbie and Raquelle go
to the fairy city.
They get fake wings.

The girls go
to the palace.
They will
save Ken.

They ride
flying ponies.

At the palace,
the duel begins.
Zane uses magic.

Ken does not
know magic.
He jumps away
from Zane.

Barbie arrives
with her friends.
Graciella traps them!

She makes Ken
ask her
to marry him.

Barbie and her friends
are trapped in orbs.

Carrie and Taylor
try to escape.
But they cannot.

Raquelle hugs Barbie.
They are friends now.
Their friendship makes
their orb burst!
It makes their
wings turn real!

Barbie and Raquelle
hurry to save Ken!

Graciella tries
to stop the girls
with magic.

with magic.

But Barbie uses
the magic
on Graciella.
The spell breaks!

Graciella is free.
She loves Zane.

Zane asks Graciella
to marry him.
She says yes.

Zane and Graciella have a fairy wedding!

Graciella is happy.
She thanks Barbie
and her friends.
She sends them home.

Now Barbie, Ken,
and Raquelle
share a fairy secret!